Bonnie's
BLUE
HOUSE

by Kelly Asbury

Henry Holt and Company

New York

Henry Holt and Company, Inc.
Publishers since 1866
115 West 18th Street
New York, New York 10011

Henry Holt is a registered trademark
of Henry Holt and Company, Inc.

Published in Canada by Fitzhenry & Whiteside Ltd.,
195 Allstate Parkway, Markham, Ontario L3R 4T8.

Library of Congress Cataloging-in-Publication Data
Asbury, Kelly.
Bonnie's blue house/Kelly Asbury.
Summary: Bonnie describes a day's activities
at home—swimming, playing in the shade, getting clean,
eating dessert, reading a story, and going to sleep.
[1. Home—Fiction] I. Title.
PZ7.A775Bo 1996 [E]—dc20 96-21715

ISBN 0-8050-4022-6
First Edition–1997
Typography by Martha Rago
The artist used water-soluble crayon on bristol board
to create the illustrations for this book.
Printed in the United States of America
on acid-free paper. ◑▬◐
10 9 8 7 6 5 4 3 2 1

For my wife, Loretta Weeks-Asbury
                                    –K. A.

I am Bonnie and this
is my cat, Bluebonnet.
She is a little shy.

This is our house.

We live here with my mom and dad

and Benny, my baby brother.

When it is hot, my friends
and I go swimming
in the backyard...

...or we play in the shade.

I go to the kitchen for a drink.

I get
clean in the
bathroom.

At dinnertime, I like dessert best!

Some nights, I
watch TV in the den.

Then, I go to sleep.